© This edition
BABY'S FIRST BOOK CLUB
Sandvik Publishing Ltd., Bristol, PA

Produced by Magi Publications, London
© 1994 Text, Linda Jennings
© 1994 Illustrations, Catherine Walters

Printed in Belgium by Proost N.V.

ISBN# 1-881445-32-1

MILLIE

By
Linda Jennings

Illustrated by
Catherine Walters

Baby's First Book Club®

Millie was a lop-eared rabbit who lived in a hutch. Her brothers and sisters munched away quite happily on their lettuce-leaves, but Millie was different.

"I want to be free," she said. But, above all, she wanted to meet a wild rabbit.

"Don't be stupid," said Billy. "Wild rabbits are *fierce.*"

"They'd eat you up," added Lily.

"They smell," said Dilly, twitching her nose.

One evening someone left the hutch door open. This was Millie's chance! With a flick of her little white tail she was off and away!

"Come back, Millie," called Billy, Dilly and Lily, but Millie took no notice.

Beyond the garden lay a big field. Millie could just see it, if she stood on her hind legs and looked through the hedge.

"That's where the wild rabbits must live," she thought. She burrowed underneath, and came out on the other side...

...where a fox was waiting for her! Millie had never seen a fox before. She stared at him, without moving. The fox licked his lips. He took a step forward...

"*Run, you stupid thing, run!*" cried a gruff voice, and suddenly the field was filled with rabbits, racing towards their burrows.

Millie didn't have time to think – she ran too.

"In here," ordered the same voice, and Millie shot right down a hole at her feet.

"That was a close one," said the wild rabbit.
"That old fox nearly had you!"

He touched Millie's nose.

"You look funny," he said. "Why are your ears
drooping down?"

"Because I'm a lop-eared rabbit," said Millie.

She thought the wild rabbit looked funny too, with
his dull grey coat and perked-up ears. He wasn't fierce,
though, and he had saved her life.

When the fox had gone, the two rabbits came up into the field again.

"I'm Seventy-Six," said the wild rabbit. "We're called by numbers because there are so many of us."

The rabbit thought Millie was a sissy name, and said so.

"You're very rude," said Millie, trying to clean the earth off her coat.

"I speak my mind," said Seventy-Six. But he didn't tell Millie she was the prettiest rabbit he'd ever seen.

The sun was setting and the field was tinged with
a rosy-pink glow. The two rabbits chased each other round
and round the oak tree and all over the field.

Seventy-Six was much faster than Millie, and she was
soon panting for breath. "I'm not used to running," she puffed.
"But isn't it wonderful to be free?"

Millie and Seventy-Six suddenly skidded to a stop.
A whole line of rabbits was sitting at the edge of the field,
staring at them.

"Don't worry," said Seventy-Six. "It's only my family."
The rabbits crowded closer.

"What's *that*?" asked one.

"It's a namby-pamby tame rabbit," said another.

"We can't have funny-looking rabbits here," said Father
rabbit. "Especially brainless
rabbits who attract foxes."

"Go back to where you
came from," snapped
Seventy-Six's uncle.

Millie looked at the unfriendly wild rabbits and trembled. Her brother Billy had been right. They did look very fierce, but she was determined not to show them she was afraid.

"All right, I'll go," she said. "See if I care!"

A big buck rabbit advanced on her with bared teeth.

"Yes, get out!" he snapped. "We don't want the likes of you here!"

He thumped the ground with his powerful back legs. Millie gave him a bold stare, turned up her little wobbly nose, and scampered back across the field.

The big buck rabbit chased her as far as the hedge.

"AND DON'T YOU DARE COME BACK AGAIN," he roared at her.

Millie dug her way back into the garden. Her heart was still beating fast. She wondered what had happened to Seventy-Six. She felt sad, because she had wanted to be friends with him.

Millie hopped back to the hutch, but the door was now locked, and Billy, Dilly and Lily fast asleep. She began to nibble at the wire, but then stopped. The hutch looked very small and dark. She remembered how miserable she had been living in it.

Millie hopped down the garden again. It
looked quite different in the dark. Shadows
moved in the bushes. A cat yeowled. Something
small scuttled across the path – and something
LARGER was coming across the lawn towards
her.

Millie was tired of being chased. As she
turned tail to run back to the hutch, a familiar
voice called out to her...

"Millie, it's me – Seventy-Six! I told them that
if they didn't want you, then I would go, too,"
he said. "And I did."

So Seventy-Six had come into the garden to find
her!

"I don't want to live in the hutch any more," said
Millie. "I want to be free, like you!"

"You don't mind living wild?" asked Seventy-Six.

"Not if we can be together," said Millie.

So Millie and Seventy-Six left the garden and the
field and travelled on to look for a new home...
... and they found one that was exactly right!

Now Millie and Seventy-Six have a very
special secret. And if you come with me, over the hill
and into the bluebell wood, you will see what it is!